MAD. OVERBOARD

Edited by ALBERT B. FELDSTEIN

WARNER BOOKS

A Warner Communications Company

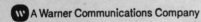

AS T. Byron Schmeer of Muncie, Indiana, once remarked to C. Fensterwick McCandless, of Hopatcong, New Jersey: "When you've seen one Barbra Streisand movie, you've seen them all!" With these immortal words ringing in our ears, we here at MAD now present, once and for all...

ON A C
YOU CA
FUNNY GI
"HELLO DOL

Hey, you kids! Bubby Strident is **singing** over the main title, and you're all **yelling** and **screaming** and **carrying on!**

Whatsa matter, Mister? Don't you ever **sing along?!**

I've seen this picture 31 times!

What on earth for?

The first time for the plot, the second time for the camera-work, and the other 29 times to **decipher** the **lyrics** when Bubby sings!

Why didn't you do what I did? I brought along an **interpreter** from Brooklyn!

ARTIST: MORT DRUCKER

AR DAY
N SEE A
SINGING
" FOREVER

I understand Bubby will be here in person tomorrow!

Where? In the lobby **signing** her autograph or on the stage **saying hello** to her fans?

In the box office **collecting** her 10% of the gross!

Enough with all these snotty remarks! The show's starting and you'd better pay attention 'cause this is the most **confusing** move satire Mad's ever done!

WRITER: FRANK JAC(

Class, I shall now demonstrate the **scientific value** of hypnosis by giving each of these subjects a **post-hypnotic suggestion** . . .
Mr. Jennings, when I clap my hands, you will awake, quack like a duck, jump like a frog, and eat like a horse . . .
Mr. Cooper, when I clap my hands you will awake, think you are an airplane, fly out the window of this 10-story building, bounce twice, and die . . .
Miss Vavoom, when I clap my hands, you will awake, go to my apartment, slip into something comfortable, and wait for me in a state of trembling ecstasy! Ah, **science**!

Ah, this student is in the **deepest** hypnotic trance I've ever seen! Who are you? And please don't sing me your answer—I want to **understand you**!

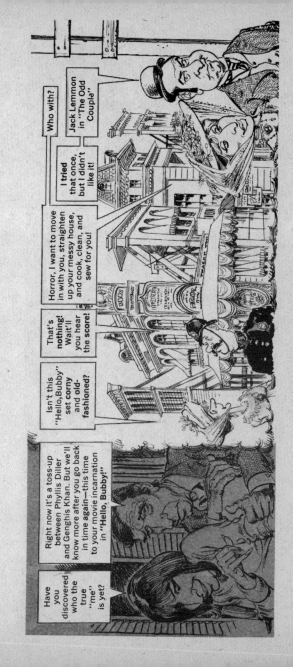

ONE DAY IN A CRASH-PAD

THE
LIGHTER
SIDE OF...
LOVE

ARTIST & WRITER: DAVE BERG

When I **first** got to college, the only thing that the boys I dated ever wanted was SEX! So I told them they could all go jump in the lake!

Good for you!

Then I met **Warren** . . . a handsome studious, gentlemanly type! And he and I started a **real, deep, meaningful relationship!**

That's nice

Nice, yes! But it was an **absolute bore!**

Why? What was **missing?**

SEX!!

Oh, Daddy! **Daddy!** I've met him **at last!** Mr. **Right!** And I'm in **love**—really in **love!**

He's my **Prince Charming** . . . my **Knight in Shining Armor!** Oh, Daddy, he's absolutely **gorgeous!** He's the most **beautiful** man I've ever met!

Well . . . let's **see** this Mr. Wonderful!

Hey, Kenny . . . come in and **show** yourself!

Oh, wow! Am I a **make-out artist**! She's **completely relaxed**! She's **surrendering** without a struggle! Gee, I must really **fascinate** her!

Gee, that **Paul Newman** really **fascinates** me!

A
COLLECTION OF

ARTIST: BOB CLARKE

MAD
X-RAYvings

WRITER: DON EDWING

Hey, gang! It's "Vacation Time" again . . . which means that "Vacation Resorts" are advertising like crazy again, too. And so, in order to keep you from being conned, thereby avoiding anger, resentment and disappointment when selecting a place for Summertime Fun, MAD now presents a simple course in

HOW TO READ A RESORT AD

ARTIST: GEORGE WOODBRIDGE   WRITER: GILBERT BARNHILL

Come spend some peaceful,

Paradise

* Dine on Gourmet Menu Meals in our Charming and Picturesque Main Lodge

* Swim at our Private, Uncrowded Beach

* Enjoy Rowing and Other Water Sports

* Commune with Nature along one of our many beautiful Scenic Hiking Trails

* Visit Points of Historic Interest nearby

PARADISE in the PINES is easy to find-

restful days at...
In The Pines

ALL OF OUR CABINS FACE THE LAKE

A FRIENDLY ATMOSPHERE PREVAILS

A COURTEOUS STAFF TO SERVE YOU

just follow the signs!

URN THE PAGE FOR MAD'S ASTUTE ANALYSIS!

peaceful, restful days

The freight trains only run on the tracks behind your cabin at night!

Dine on Gourmet Menu Meals

... except that we're always out of everything on the menu but the Hamburger and the "Chef's Surprise"!

Commune with Nature

We're plagued with spiders and wasps!

Charming and Picturesque Main Lodge

It hasn't been painted or repaired for years!

ALL OF OUR CABINS FACE THE LAKE

. . . which is a good two miles down the road!

Swim at our Private, Uncrowded Beach

It's "Uncrowded" because the water's polluted!

A FRIENDLY ATMOSPHERE PREVAILS

The cabins are only five feet apart!

Scenic Hiking Trails

. . . to the "Johns", other facilities, and the fancy resort next door!

A COURTEOUS STAFF TO SERVE YOU

If you can find one of them!

Enjoy Rowing and Other Water Sports

Mostly after the frequent flash floods!

Visit Points of Historic Interest nearby

Mainly, "Souvenir Stands" and other "Tourist Traps"

easy to find—just follow the signs!

They're all along the "old" highway!

IN A SPECIALIST'S

OFFICE

You Know You're REALLY A FOOTBALL FAN When...

ARTIST: JACK DAVIS

WRITER: STAN HART

You Know You're REALLY A FOOTBALL FAN When . . .

. . . you discover your wife is having an affair,
but you don't want to make anything out of it
because it gets her out of the house on Sundays.

You Know You're REALLY A FOOTBALL FAN When . . .

. . . you miss the Monday morning funeral of a close relative
because you're too broken up over your team's loss on Sunday

You Know You're REALLY A FOOTBALL FAN When . . .

. . . it really matters to you who wins the "AFL—All-Pro Bowl Game."

You Know You're REALLY A FOOTBALL FAN When . . .

. . . you sit and stare at the TV set from February to July because you just can't believe that the "G.E. College Bowl" isn't some sort of post-season game.

You Know You're REALLY A FOOTBALL FAN When . . .

. . . you stay up nights memorizing the numbers of the Kick-off and the Kick-return teams.

You Know You're REALLY A FOOTBALL FAN When . . .

. . . you rediscover a childhood prayer because your team is two points behind with six seconds left.

You Know You're REALLY A FOOTBALL FAN When . . .

. . . you refuse to consider divorcing
your wife because you're afraid she'll
get custody of your season tickets.

You Know You're REALLY A FOOTBALL FAN When . . .

. . . you go to the home of people you
hate because they have a color TV set.

You Know You're REALLY A FOOTBALL FAN When . . .

. . . you arrange your Summer vacation so you'll be able to attend the "College All-Star—Pro Game" in July.

You Know You're REALLY A FOOTBALL FAN When . . .

. . . you make $195 a week, and you think O.J. Simpson got a "raw deal" because he's only getting $400,000.

You Know You're REALLY A FOOTBALL FAN When . . .

. . . you buy a house at least 75 miles away so you can see the home games that are blacked out in the city.

You Know You're REALLY A FOOTBALL FAN When . . .

. . . you ask the crowd to be quiet so you can hear the sportscaster on your portable radio describe the play you just saw.

You Know You're REALLY A FOOTBALL FAN When . . .

. . . you make sure you get home by 11 P.M.
Sunday night so you can see the highlights
of the game you were at that afternoon.

You Know You're REALLY A FOOTBALL FAN When . . .

. . . you learn your wife just had a baby because
they announce it over the public address system.

The Psychology Of Snoring

WRITER: FRANK JACOBS

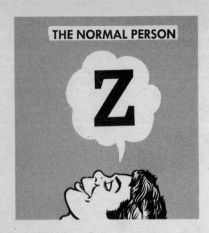

The Psychotic

THE PATRIOT

THE SADIST

THE EXTROVERT

The Neurotic

THE MASOCHIST

Hey, gang! It's time once again for MAD's nutty old "Cliché Monster" game. Here's how it works: Take any familiar phrase or colloquial expression, give it an eerie setting so you create a new-type monster, and you're playing it. Mainly, you're—

HORRIF

Embracing A BELIEF

YING CLICHÉS

ARTIST: PAUL COKER, JR.   WRITER: MAY SAKAMI

Introducing A RESOLUTION

Avoiding A CONFRONTATION

Weighing An ALTERNATIVE

Fishing For A COMPLIMENT

Grilling A SUSPECT

Filing A RETURN

Swinging A DEAL

Tickling A FANCY

Controlling An IMPULSE

Developing A TECHNIQUE

Posing A PROBLEM

Receiving A STANDING OVATION

Scrapping A PROJECT

Serving A SUMMONS

Pouring Oil On TROUBLED WATERS

ONE DAY IN THE GARDEN OF EDEN

HAVING TROUBLE WITH YOUR PARENTS?
MAYBE YOU CAN WIN YOUR ARGUMENT
BY CONVINCING THEM YOU'RE RIGHT
WITH ONE OF THESE

MAD CLIPPINGS TO LEAVE LYING AROUND

WRITER: ALPHONSE NORMANDIA

DATES FOR PRE-TEEN GIRLS URGED BY PROMINENT SCIENTIST

NEW YORK, N.Y., Apr. 7—Dr. Sidney J. Sternwallow, Director of Physiology of the New York Pre-Pubescent Institute, today recommended that Mothers urge their pre-teen girls to have dates.

"Dates are extremely beneficial to a pre-teen girl's feeling of well-being," stated Dr. Sternwallow in a speech before the National Association of Pre-Pubescent Nutritionists.

"Figs, prunes and dried apricots are also very good," he went on to say. "You can't beat their natural laxative effect!"

President Recommends Higher Allowances For Young People

Higher allowances for young people was recommended as a partial solution to one of the biggest problems besetting our nation today.

"Higher allowances are necessary and vital, and should be given to our young people whether parents can afford them or not!", the President of

the National Association of Recording Companies, stated today.

"After all, kids buy 90% of all the records manufactured," he went on, "so it stands to reason that if they have more money to spend, they'll buy more records. And if they buy more records, we might recover from this terrible business slump that has hit the Recording Industry as well as practically every other industry in America!"

Teenagers Who Have Their Own Telephones Suffer From Less Hang-Ups

"If you want your child to have less hang-ups, get him his own phone!" states a survey report released today.

The report noted that teenagers who have their own telephones suffer from far less hang-ups than teenagers who share their phones with others.

The survey, conducted recently by the Bell System, showed that teenagers who have their own telephones talk for long periods of time, uninterrupted, while those who share phones with their families are forced to hang up much more often.

Scientist Proves Long, Unkempt Hair Beneficial To Health

Professor Henry L. Cranston, of the University of Southern North Carolina, spoke out today in support of long hair.

In an address before the staid Alumni Association of U.S.N.C., Prof. Cranston claimed that he possesses indisputable proof that life is actually prolonged by long, straggly hair.

The Professor based his claim on his forty-year study of the Long-Haired Alaskan Musk Ox, an animal native to the Northern-most Polar Zones.

"Just suppose the Musk Ox had short hair," Prof. Cranston suggested. "The poor things would freeze to death!"

2-Hour School Day Urged by Educators

Leading Educators, in a special meeting here today, expressed concern over long, and for the most part, useless hours spent in school by students.

"It's really ridiculous," said one teacher. "The attention span of all students is normally limited. After an hour or so, it's no use trying to teach them anything!"

The teachers signed a resolution recommending a 2-hour school day, including a half-hour lunch break, be adopted as sufficient for effective learning.

At the conclusion of the meeting, the group returned to their teaching assignments at the Gladstone Obedience Training School For Dogs.

After-School Chores Seen As Damaging

"Assigning after-school chores to a boy or girl instead of allowing the child to play may result in irreparable damage!" stated Dr. Hugo Youngfroyd, the noted Child Psychologist.

"But the damage to grass, windows, dishes, etc. caused by the child's unconscious resentment of having to meet mature responsibilities is little price to pay for the character building that results.

"If you can afford the cost of replacing a dish broken while washing, or a window smashed while cleaning, or a lawn torn up by cutting, or a car destroyed while polishing, make the little stinkers work," concluded Dr. Youngfroyd.

HOMEWORK CAUSES BRAIN DAMAGE

In another of a rapidly growing series of incidents, a student's brain which may well indicate a serious trend, a result of homework. was irreparably damaged as a result of homework.

"There is no doubt that the student's extremely heavy work-study load was directly responsible for the brain damage," stated Dean Roger Hornsby of the University of Biloxi Medical School, "and we are going to have to severely limit the use of homework to meet that load."

However, it is quite possible that the damage to the brain could have been avoided!"

John J. Fazool, a Pre-Med student at the University, had brought home a calf's brain he had been dissecting in Comparative Mammalia Lab. Class. Mrs. Emilio Fazool, his mother, mistakenly cooked the brain and served it to the Fazool family for dinner.

"It was a little tough," said Mrs. Fazool, "but I covered it with a creamed garlic gravy and smothered it with capers and anchovies and it was simply delicious!"

NOTED EDUCATOR CLAIMS THAT HIGHEST MARKS IN SCHOOL ARE MOST OFTEN PRODUCED BY LEAST INTELLIGENT PUPILS

EAST FLEEGLE, Mo., March 5—Students who make high marks in school were criticized today, while low mark students were praised by East Fleegle High School Principal, Harvey Streech.

"Some of our most brilliant and intellectually superior students are low markers," stated Mr. Streech, "while high marks most often indicate a student of base mentality, if not total stupidity!"

Principal Streech's remarks were made following the High School's annual Spring cleanup of wall defacements and obscenity scrawls.

"It's pretty obvious that the more intelligent students are empathetic to our clean-up problem, and make their marks relatively low, where it is easy for the school custodian to wash them off. But the high markers, often the most vile and obscene, can't even be reached by ladder. It's a mystery to me how those morons can deface a ceiling!"

ADULTS OVER 25 ARE LABELED AS 'UNSAFE DRIVERS'

"Sixty-seven percent of all men and women over 25 driving an automobile on the road today are unsafe drivers!", claimed Professor Chester Fiduciary in a speech before the National Insurance Underwriters Assn. today.

"The reason" stated Professor Fiduciary, "that such a high percentage of adults over 25 are unsafe drivers is because that's how many are going to be smashed into by drivers who are *under 25!*

CONTINUED SHOWERS AND BATHS EXTREMELY HAZARDOUS TO HEALTH

Dr. Etoin Shrdlu, prominent Psycho-Physicist, reported today that "the continued taking of showers and baths can be extremely hazardous to health!"

In a speech before the American Psycho-Physical Society, Dr. Shrdlu also claimed that the life expectancy of a regular showerer or bather will be considerably shortened if the practice were to be continued.

"Indeed, severe bodily damage is almost a certainty," he stated flatly, "and death is a distinct possibility!"

Dr. Shrdlu, who is connected with NASA's "Office of Space Medicine," went on to say that "any Astronaut who insisted upon taking a shower or a bath while exploring the surface of the Moon would have to remove his pressurized space suit. Not only would this be extremely hazardous, but it would also tend to make him look a little ridiculous on television!"

Ever since we published "The MAD Hate Book" a few issues back, we've been receiving an enormous trickle of mail which says (in essence): "Don't you clods knows there's

THE MAD

DON'T YOU JUST LOVE . . .

. . . getting up early for school, and suddenly remembering it's Saturday!

ARTIST: PAUL COKER, JR.

too much hate in the world? Stop emphasizing it! We hate you for it! Why not show the good things in life?" And so, after reflecting on some of life's sunnier moments, we now present...

LOVE
BOOK

DON'T YOU JUST LOVE...

... finishing a picture puzzle!

WRITER: GEORGE HART

DON'T YOU JUST LOVE . . .

. . . being pampered while sick in bed!

DON'T YOU JUST LOVE . . .

. . . squishing mud through your toes!

DON'T YOU JUST LOVE . . .

. . . reading your name in the newspaper!

DON'T YOU JUST LOVE . . .

. . . making a good trade!

DON'T YOU JUST LOVE . . .

. . . being told you look
younger than you really are!

DON'T YOU JUST LOVE . . .

. . . finding a parking meter with time left on it!

DON'T YOU JUST LOVE . . .

. . . the smell of a new car!

DON'T YOU JUST LOVE . . .

. . . having a good friend who's big!

DON'T YOU JUST LOVE . . .

. . . opening a jar no one else can!

DON'T YOU JUST LOVE . . .

. . . when your teacher gets sick
on the day of the big test!

DON'T YOU JUST LOVE . . .

. . . getting a birthday card containing cash!

DON'T YOU JUST LOVE . . .

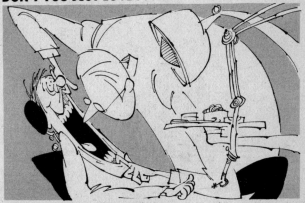

. . . going to the dentist and being
told all you need is a cleaning!

DON'T YOU JUST LOVE . . .

. . . cracking the ice on puddles!

DON'T YOU JUST LOVE . . .

. . . finding money in a pay phone slot!

DON'T YOU JUST LOVE . . .

. . . getting a free sample of something!

DON'T YOU JUST LOVE . . .

. . . meeting someone from your graduating
class who looks much older than you!

DON'T YOU JUST LOVE . . .

. . . getting flowers!

DON'T YOU JUST LOVE . . .

. . . getting a surprise in your lunch box!

DON'T YOU JUST LOVE . . .

. . . when nobody else wants
the last piece of pizza!

DON'T YOU JUST LOVE . . .

. . . when told you look
older than you really are!

DON'T YOU JUST LOVE . . .

. . . having your back scratched!

DON'T YOU JUST LOVE . . .

. . . discovering money in an old pocket!

Hey, gang! Here we go again in our never-ending quest for new inspirations for Hollywood "Horror Films".

This time, MAD suggests that Producers of these bombs can create...

NEW MOVIE MONSTERS

from the MEDICAL WORLD

ARTIST: JACK RICKARD

WRITER: E. NELSON BRIDWELL

THEY CAME BY DAY ... THEY CAME BY NIGHT ...
DRAWING THE BLOOD FROM THEIR VICTIM'S VEINS!
*And when it came time to operate, they
put it all back ... and charged for it!*

"THE BLOOD-TEST VAMPIRES"

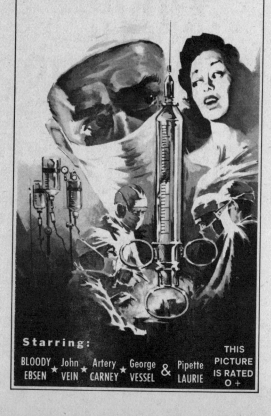

Starring:

BLOODY EBSEN ★ John VEIN ★ Artery CARNEY ★ George VESSEL & Pipette LAURIE

THIS PICTURE IS RATED O+

WHY DID THE SADISTIC WHITE SPECTRE WAKE HIM
FROM A FITFUL SLEEP AT THE STROKE OF TWELVE?
★ ★ ★ ★ ★ ★ ★ ★ ★ ★ ★ ★ ★ ★ ★ ★ ★ ★
WHAT AWFUL THINGS DID SHE FORCE HIM TO SWALLOW?
★ ★ ★ ★ ★ ★ ★ ★ ★ ★ ★ ★ ★ ★ ★ ★ ★ ★
SEE THE NURSE, WITH HIS MEDICINE, SUBJECT HIM TO

"THE
COLD HAND
AT MIDNIGHT"

WHAT WAS IT THAT...
FRIGHTENED POLITICIANS—
TERRIFIED BUSINESSMEN—
PANICKED THE WHOLE A.M.A.?

IT WAS...

"THE MENACE OF MEDICARE!"

WITH

HY INCOME	DEE SEEVER	HARPO CONDRIAC	OLDEN SICK
as the Doctor who padded his claims	as the Nurse who raised her rates	as the Patient who sponged off the Government	as the Needy Man caught in a tangle of red tape

HE RANG AND RANG AND RANG! HE CRIED OUT
TIME AND TIME AND TIME AGAIN! BUT NO ONE
CAME! WHAT WAS THE AWFUL ANSWER TO . . .

"THE MYSTERY OF THE VANISHING NURSE"

ONE NIGHT

IN THE

ACME RITZ CENTRAL ARMS

WALDORF PLAZA STATLER

HILTON GRAND HOTEL

ORDURE OF THE DAY

It's true, as we've heard wise men say,
That every dog must have his day,
In cities, though, each day we rue
How many dogs have had their do.

The streets are spattered all through town
With beagle beige and boxer brown;
Though litter we're taught not to strew,
Still every dog's allowed his do.

ARTIST: PAUL COKER, JR.

WRITER: RONNIE NATHAN

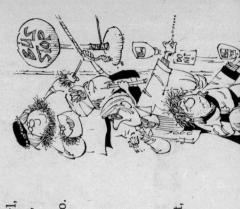

The tree-lined parks give off a scent
Of, mainly, canine excrement,
Which clings to him who wears the shoe
That steps where dogs have had their do.

In playgrounds were the toddlers crawl,
And ball fields where boys bat the ball,
Too often what will spoil the view
Are spots where Spot has stopped to do.

Our cities will soon go to seed
With droppings from the pedigreed,
From cocker, collie, Kerry blue,
And other curs who can and do.

It's not man's best friend who's at fault,
No, it's his master we must halt;
Our neighbor who expects us to
Love him and love his doggie-do.

The city's for the birds unless
We clear its grounds of hounds that mess,
And curb, instead, pet-owners who
Care little where their dogs make do.

Let's have them, like good parents, toil
At cleaning up their puppy's soil,
Removing every tell-tale clue,
Or we'll go to the dogs with do.

Have you noticed how confused the world has become lately? You have? That figures! If you weren't confused to begin with, you wouldn't be reading this trash. Still, it's our opinion (and you know what that's worth!) that one of the most confusing problems of all is today's "Drug Scene". Here at MAD, most of us like to get high on halvah and Chinese fortune cookies. We like it that way. But the fact still remains that there is a serious drug problem in this country, and it's getting worse with every sniff, puff and fix. As always, MAD is ready to help. So, adding a touch of chaos to the present ridiculous confusion, we now bring you . . .

THE MAD BLOW-YOUR-MIND DRUG PRIMER

ARTIST: BOB CLARKE   WRITER: SY REIT

Chapter 1.

See the pretty plant.
It is a Marihuana plant.
The Latin name for it is "cannabis sativa."
It is also called "pot," "tea," "gage,"
　　　"boo" and "Maryjane."
Would you like to grow this pretty plant in your garden?
If you do, you will soon have a visit from the police.
They are also called "cops," "fuzz," "narcos,"
　　　"pigs" and "the man."
When they see your garden, you will be arrested.
This is also called being "hauled in," "pinched,"
　　　"nabbed," "cribbed," and "busted."
What fun it is to learn new words!
Who would ever think that gardening could be so educational!

Chapter 2.

See the Mayor.
He is very angry.
He is angry because there is a serious
        drug problem in his town.
He blames the whole thing on today's parents.
He believes today's parents are indifferent and irresponsible.
An hour ago, three teenagers were arrested for "Possession."
See the Mayor blow his stack at today's irresponsible parents.
If you think he's angry now, wait till he finds out
        that the three teenagers are his own kids!

Chapter 3.

See the junkie.
He is waiting for his connection.
The connection is very important to the junkie.
The connection gives the junkie what he desperately needs.
The connection slips the junkie a little "magic something"
    that will make his life serene and beautiful.
See the policeman.
He is also waiting for his connection.
The connection is very important to the policeman.
The connection gives the policeman what he desperately needs.
The connection slips the policeman a little "magic something"
    that will make his life serene and beautiful.
See the connection?

Chapter 4.

See the young man.
He is sitting in a prison cell.
See how very sad he looks.
Sad, sad, sad.
Why is the young man cooped up in jail?
He is serving a 20-year sentence.
He got busted for smoking marihuana.
See the young man's cellmate.
See how very mean he looks.
Mean, mean, mean.
Why is the mean cellmate cooped up in jail?
The mean cellmate is only serving a 10-year sentence.
All he did was commit arson, rape, and a few assorted murders.

Chapter 5.

See the other young man.
His name is Elwood.
Elwood loves to travel by air.
Can he afford expensive airline tickets?
Of course not . . . but who needs planes?
Elwood just sucks on a sugar cube of LSD . . . and takes off!
Some day, when Elwood is on LSD
He will zoom right off the roof.
Crash, crash, crash.
Bye-bye, Elwood.
LSD is swell for flying.
The trouble is, it's not much good for landing.

Chapter 6.

See the nice, middle-class parents.
Hear them groaning and screaming.
Yarrgh, yarrgh, yarrgh.
Why are they in such a state of yarrgh?
They have just learned that their teenage son smokes pot.
Nice, middle-class parents do not approve of pot.
No, no, no.
They are against young people using drugs.
The whole idea of their son using drugs is very upsetting to them.
It is so upsetting, they will have to double their usual dose
      of tranquilizers and sleeping pills today.

Chapter 7.

See the shiftless drug addict.
He has no home. He has no money. He has no ambition.
All he wants is to be left alone to do his own thing.
Shame on the shiftless drug addict.
He is downright un-American!
See the mighty Mafia chief.
He has wealth. He has power. He has ambition.
Every year, he squeezes millions of dollars out of
    poor, sick, helpless drug addicts.
The mighty Mafia chief is a real go-getter.
Three cheers for the mighty Mafia chief.
Thank goodness there are some people who still know
    what this great country of ours stands for!

Chapter 8.

See the Senator.
The Senator is making an important speech.
It is a speech against legalizing marihuana.
The Senator has strong ideas about drugs.
In his opinion, all drugs are reprehensible.
He points out that drugs can be harmful to the human body.
Harmful, harmful, harmful.
Why does the Senator look so shaky and glassy-eyed?
You'd be shaky and glassy-eyed too
If you had as many martinis for lunch as he did!

Chapter 9.

See the nice freaked-out Hippie couple.
The nice, freaked-out Hippie couple does everything together.
They smoke hash together.
They drop acid together.
They shoot heroin together.
They take mescaline, cocaine, "speed" and "bennies" together.
They experiment with all kinds of crazy drugs together.
When the baby comes, they will take care of it together.
And they will name it together.
What will the nice, freaked-out couple name their new baby?
That all depends . . .
On whether the baby is a "he"—a "she"—or an "IT"!

Chapter 10.

See the busy Drug Rehabilitation Center.
It is crowded with suffering drug addicts.
Crowded, crowded, crowded.
They have been waiting all day to get a little help.
But, alas, there aren't enough beds to go around
And there aren't enough doctors to go around.
And there aren't enough social workers to go around.
And there aren't enough psychiatrists to go around.
Where does all the money go that is voted for Drug Rehabilitation?
That's easy!
It goes to Federal and State Commissions
    that investigate *why* there aren't enough beds
        or doctors or social workers or psychiatrists to go around!

THE
LIGHTER
SIDE OF...
BO

Do you realize that there are **five oceans**—covering **7/10ths** of the Earth's **surface**! The **Atlantic Ocean** alone covers **31,530,000** square miles! And the **Pacific** covers **63,800,000** square miles!

Add to **that** all of the lakes, rivers and bays . . . and it means that **¾ of the entire world** is covered with **water**!

ATING

ARTIST & WRITER: DAVE BERG

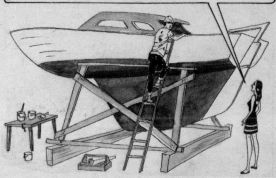

So long, Mom! I'm leaving now to spend the day on Norman's boat!

Hey, did you take your **pill?**

PILL?!? Oh, my **God!!**

What kind of wild orgies do you **have** on that boat of yours?!

Oh, Mother! Not **that** kind of pill! You've got a **dirty mind!** Norman is talking about an **anti-sea-sickness** pill!

Well, **that's** a relief!!

But thanks for **reminding** me!!

Let's face it! **One** of the reasons we buy **bigger** and bigger boats is to **impress** our boating friends!

And one of the gimmicks we use to let people **know** we've moved up to a bigger boat is to **keep the same name** but put a **number** after it!

My **first** boat, "The Rover," cost me **$7000**! But compared to the **others**, it was a **dink**! So I moved up to "**Rover II**"! That one cost me **$14,000**!

The **following** year, I bought "**Rover III**" for **$21,000**! And now . . . this year—

I know! You bought "**Rover IV**"!

Except that I decided to give it **another** name! This year, I decided to call a spade a spade!

$34,789.⁵⁹

ONE MORNING IN THE LIFE OF AN OPTICIAN

A MAD LOOK AT... OBEDIENCE TRAINING

Since an unruly dog can be a pest, and a well-trained dog can be a wonderful companion, the "Obedience School For Dogs" has become very popular lately. However, the same can be said for kids! Since an unruly child can be a pest, and a well-trained child can be a joy . . .

ARTIST & WRITER: DEAN NORMAN

WHY NOT "OBEDIENCE SCHOOLS FOR KIDS"?

Wouldn't it be great if we could train kids to obey a few simple commands, such as . . .

AND WHY NOT "OBEDIENCE SCHOOLS FOR HUSBANDS"?

AND WHY NOT "OBEDIENCE SCHOOLS FOR WIVES"?!?

As we all know, the Hippies, the Yippies, the SDS, the Black Panthers, and just about every activist group in the country has its own newspaper. Yes, the Underground Press is flourishing with such publications as "The East Village Other," "The Berkeley Barb," as well as other titles too numerous to mention, as well as still other titles we wouldn't dare mention! Well, whether you know it or not, the enemy is starting to fight back. Ever since Spiro Agnew came along, and Time Magazine named "The Middle American" as "Man of the Year," the pendulum has begun to swing in the other direction. So, Underground Press—Beware! Watch out for things to come—like THE OVERGROUND PRESS, and sickening publications like

SILENT

The Magazine for

"I CLAWED MY WAY TO THE TOP —WHY CAN'T THOSE OTHER PUNK KIDS?"
by David Eisenhower

★ ★ ★

"I Moved Out of Montana When A Negro Family Moved In Next Door— In Idaho!"

★ ★ ★

"Make War, Not Love"
The heart-warming memoirs of General Westmoreland

★ ★ ★

"Is Jim Nabors Too Controversial For Prime-time Television?"
by Lawrence Welk

★ ★ ★

"SEX: A Time and a Place For it"
Part 6 of the 10 part series deals with

"SHALL WE WAIT TILL WE'RE MARRIED TO KISS?"

★ ★ ★

"Don't be afraid to beat the Ten Commandments into your kids!"

MAJORITY

iddle America   50¢

(Each penny of which says, "In God We Trust" and those Commie kids better believe it!)

SPECIAL BONUS OFFER:
A Genuine 33 RPM record entitled, "PAT BOONE SINGS HAPPY ENDINGS TO JOAN BAEZ'S PROTEST SONGS"

"SILENT SAYS"

Each month, editor Sam Silent answers questions and tries to solve problems submitted by our readers.

Dear Silent:
I find it hard to tell one Cabinet member from another. In fact I heard a rumor the other day that you'll never see Sect. of State Rogers and Attorney General Mitchell photographed together because they're the same man. Is this true?

Brandon Edwing
Spokane, Washington

Dear Mr. Edwing:
I checked the rumor out with Sect. of Defense Laird (or as he is laughingly referred to by his friends—"Sect. of the Treasury Kennedy") and he said "That's ridiculous. They're talking about Sect. of Health, Education and Welfare FINCH!"

Dear Silent:
I think those anti-war demonstrators should be tarred and feathered. I think we should do all we can to help our boys in Vietnam. We send them letters and food packages and every Christmas Bob Hope goes to see them with Ann-Margret, Pamela Tiffin, and Raquel Welch. And yet when I see the boys on TV, they look disturbed. Why are they disturbed?

Grace Warbler
Mamaroneck, N.Y.

Dear Miss Warbler:
They're disturbed because every Christmas Bob Hope goes to see them with Ann-Margret, Pamela Tiffin, and Raquel Welch.

Dear Silent:
As a decent Middle American, I, like you and the editors of this magazine, do not believe in prejudice (only last month I swam in the same Pacific Ocean the Mexicans were swimming in). Which is why I find those Polish jokes that are going around so offensive. Some of our finest citizens are Polish-Americans. Who started those Polish jokes anyway?

Oliver Brack
Los Angeles, Cal.

Dear Mr. Brack:
It could have been a recalcitrant college youth, or perhaps an effusive monologist with a sense of perverse levity. And then again it might have been some Wop.

Dear Silent:
I have just returned from the South Pole, where I spent the last 10 years, and I feel a little out of touch with things. I'm looking for a new career to go into and I'm considering that of a College Policeman. I think it would be splendid to patrol a nice, friendly campus, smile a cheery hello at the students, and call them by name while they address me warmly by mine. What do you think of my idea?

James Pigg
Sioux City, Iowa

Dear Mr. Pigg:
Have you ever considered going into the plumbing business?

Dear Silent:
As a conscientious Middle American citizen living in Wyoming, I thought it might be a good idea to bring the world a little closer to my children. So next Christmas, instead of taking them to Disneyland again, I thought I would take them to look at a Negro. Can you help me? What do Negroes look like? Where do I find one? Are they friendly? Is it a good idea to feed them? Do they bite?

Ned Womber
Laramie, Wyoming

Dear Mr. Womber:
I admire your wonderful plan and think you have an excellent idea. However, I don't think you are ready for it just yet. I suggest you do something as traumatic as that GRADUALLY! Instead of jumping right in, and possibly "over your head," why not BUILD UP to a Negro by taking your children to see a Jew first?

STATUS QUO-TES

Our roving cameraman gets opinions on the burning issues of the day from random Middle Americans. This month's question:

"How do you feel about today's attitudes towards sex?"

Fred Sashay, Fire Island, N.Y.

I don't pay much attention to today's attitudes towards sex. *My* attitude towards sex has been the same since I was four. My mummsy took care of that. But I can't complain—I've got a good interior decorating business going and my sweetheart and I recently rented a beautiful new apartment which we will move into as soon as his divorce comes through.

Harry Trefflick, Salem, Oregon

Maybe I'm a little different from most people in my generation, but I'm all for this new freedom of sexual expression for kids. I've always encouraged my son Ted to bring girls home to the house, ever since he was 15. Now that Ted is older and off to college, I miss him. I also miss the girls he used to bring home. Now if I can only think of a way to get my *wife* off to college!

Caleb Flint, Saginaw, Michigan

I think today's attitudes are disgusting. These kids are sick. We're raising a generation of perverts. I'd like to string up a few by there thumbs and whip 'em. But not just an ordinary whip. No, a nice, freshly oiled whip that's laid across their shoulders in clean, even strokes, until their skin welts and a little blood wells up in the gashes. That'll teach those sickies a little decency.

Paul (Pop) Armbruster, St. Petersburgh, Fla.

I'm glad you stopped me, young feller. Yes sir, always like to talk to folks. I'm just 84 years young and still the picture of health. Would you believe it, my mind's still as quick as a steel trap. Yes sir, I can remember clear back to the Blizzard of '88. Course I don't remember recent things too well. Now then, concerning your question . . . what's *sex?*

Every month this magazine awards 10,000 Red, White, and Blue Stamps to the fiction piece which best mirrors the clean, decent, patriotic thoughts of today's Middle American. We are pleased to present this month's winning story.

DICK DECENT,
College Student

"Like to go for a walk, Jane?" said Dick Decent to his coed girl friend Jane Wasp, as they met on the campus of State Agricultural College. She nodded cheerily and they began to stroll.

Dick was a clean-cut, handsome lad of 19. He had a neat crew-cut and wore a red and white tennis sweater and white buckskin shoes. Jane, a lovely, fresh-looking girl of 18, had long, neat hair and wore a simple, fresh-laundered pinafore with a tiny American flag sewn in the upper left hand corner near her heart. Together they looked like any two, plain, average, ordinary, American college students.

"What a great day it is," said Dick. "And what a grand school this is, and how lucky we both are to be here. Golly!"

"Dick, must you use *profanity?*" said Jane.

"Sorry," said Dick.

"Oh, look," said Jane, "there go some ROTC cadets."

"How tall and strong they look," said Dick. "What a great bunch of fellows."

"They send a tingle of pride up and down my spine," said Jane.

"I doubt if anyone on campus is more beloved by the student body than they are," said Dick simply, as a tear of joy crept out of his eye. He quickly brushed it away.

"Oh, say, Jane," said Dick, "would you like to go to the Prom with me?"

"I'd like to, Dick," said Jane, "but..."

"I'm sorry about last night, Jane," said Dick. "I didn't mean to do what I did."

"It's not that I don't *want* you to kiss me," said Jane. "And I realize that there must be at least four or maybe five 'fast' girls on this campus who *do* kiss. It's just that I'm saving my kisses for Mr. Right."

At that moment along came Chancellor Valleyforge accompanied by another man.

"Hello, Dick and Jane," said the Chancellor.

"Hi, Chancellor," said Dick. "Classes are better than ever these days and we have *you* to thank for it."

"Pshaw, Dick," said the Chancellor. "I'm only doing my job. It's a pleasure working for you wholesome kids. By the way, Dick and Jane, I'd like you both to meet Mr. Eric Novotney, of the Dow Chemical Company."

"Mr. Novotney," said Jane, wringing the man's hand, "I can't tell you how proud we students here are of the wonderful job you're doing for our nation."

"Love your napalm," added Dick sincerely.

"We hope you'll join our company after you graduate, Dick," said Mr. Novotney.

"Nothing would give me more pleasure," said Dick, "but first I must go to Vietnam."

"If the Army will only have me," he added hopefully.

"What a nice man he seems (Continued on Page 53)

Along Middle America Avenue

by GRAY LIFESTYLE, JR.

Let's hear it for the congregation of Furd Township Church, Maryland. For the past eight Sundays they've given up services to picket the Supreme Court Building over the school prayer ruling. Atta-way, Furd Township! Let's get prayers out of the church and back into the public schools where they belong . . . Bad news and good news and bad news from Hominygrits, Georgia. Mel Duff, County Chicken Plucker, was just fired. Now for the good news. Mel has decided to throw all his experience behind his candidacy for Governor. Now for the bad news again. The new state constitution for Georgia dictates that a former chicken plucker cannot succeed a former chicken restaurant owner as Governor of the state. So now it looks like Mel may have to settle for the Supreme Court. You can't win 'em all . . .

* * * * * *

Tragedy Department: Friends of Hattie McLish were shocked to learn of her untimely death due to an overdose of sleeping pills. They say she'd been very despondent lately because she found out her children were taking drugs . . . Attention critics of Pres. Nixon who have been complaining about spending $26 billion to put a man on the moon instead of using that money to wipe out poverty. We've got news for you pinkos: There _is_ no poverty on the moon . . . Trouble comes in double doses: Silent Majorityite Sandra Debbs was not only heartbroken to discover that her maid just left her, she also found out that her teenage children ran away from home last Christmas.

Three cheers for Dan and Philomene Humbolt of Biloxi, Mississippi, who have been educating their children at home since the Supreme Court school desegregation ruling in 1954. The Humbolt's oldest boy, 24 year old Donald, is already up to long division, and 23 year old daughter Billie Mae hardly moves her lips anymore when she reads . . . Soon-to-wed, hard-working D.A. Ed Shtarp has been so busy lately confiscating "I Am Curious—Yellow," "Medium Cool," and other filthy films being exhibited in his county that he was almost late for those fabulous showgirls perfoming at his stag party last Friday night!

* * * * * *

How about a word of praise for those patriots at Disneyland who refuse admittance to punk kids with long hair and silly mod clothes. Said Asst. Disneyland Manager Walt Lancer (in the "Goofy" costume on the left), "If they can't look like civilized human beings we don't want 'em in here!"

It looks like Spiro's pressure campaign against the TV networks is paying off. Following Pres. Nixon's next address to the nation, instead of a critical analysis, CBS has agreed to present a 15 minute program containing "The Best of Hee Haw" . . . It's a brand new six pound baby for the Felix Ungers. He's head of the National Clean Morals Committee and she's a noted anti-nudity crusader in Wesselville, Arizona. Obeying its parents wishes, the baby was born fully clothed. Keep an eye on this column in late 1983 for word of the baby's s-x!

THE ESTABLISHMENT IN ACTION

A Pictorial Run-Down of

What's What in Middle Americas-ville

ACCIDENTS WILL HAPPEN: Was ULCA campus cop Bull Bernie's face red the other day! That large group he thought was radical campus demonstrators and which he hosed, clubbed, and sprayed with Mace, turned out to be the Establishment's own lovable King Family who were showing up on campus to do an Arbor Day concert. Try not to worry about it, Bull. You'll have real fun next Friday afternoon when the Black Students Union have their meeting!

MIDDLE AMERICAN OF THE MONTH: Cheers to Henry Cotter and his wife Wilma, who are working side by side, building for the future by drawing from the past, like all Middle Americans. They are instilling the ideals they grew up with—Clean Living, Hard Work and Our Country, Right or Wrong—into their own children, with fantastic success. The Cotters are (l. to r.): Henry, Wilma, their 15 year old daughter Nancy, and Spiro. Their 12-year-old son Henry, Jr. wasn't available for our staff photographer, having run away from home the week before.

RALLY ROUND THE FLAG: American Legion Post #23, in Canton, Ohio, had a great Americanism rally Saturday night. Although scheduled keynote speaker "Chub" Freely couldn't make it because he's up on a drunken driving charge, and Hank Endicott is laid up with cirrhosis of the liver after his recent 19 day bourbon binge, the rally was still a great success. The theme of the rally was "Let's get pot out of our highschools before our kids ruin themselves."

EXTREME DEDICATION: Our hats are off to the dedicated parents of School District #53 in Wilkes Barre, Pennsylvania. They have been holding regular meetings to try and determine ways to improve school conditions in their area. No solutions yet, but the group will meet again Thursday, right after they're expected to vote down the new school appropriations bond issue for the seventh time in over two years.